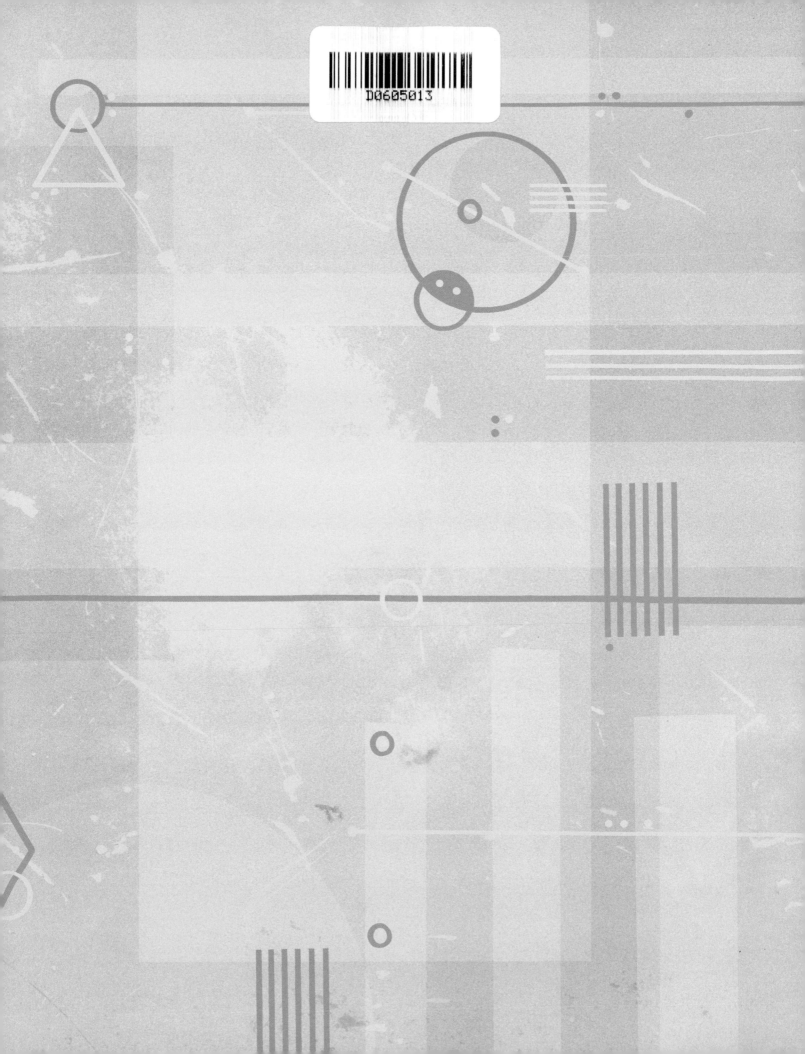

D0605013

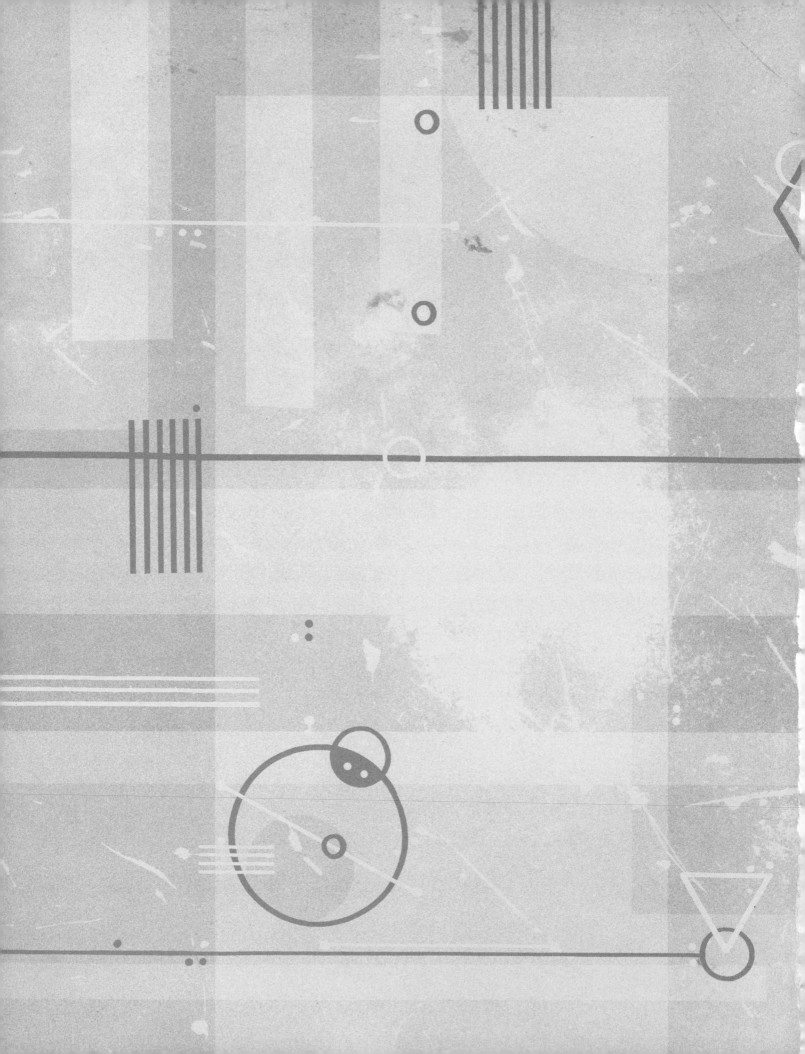

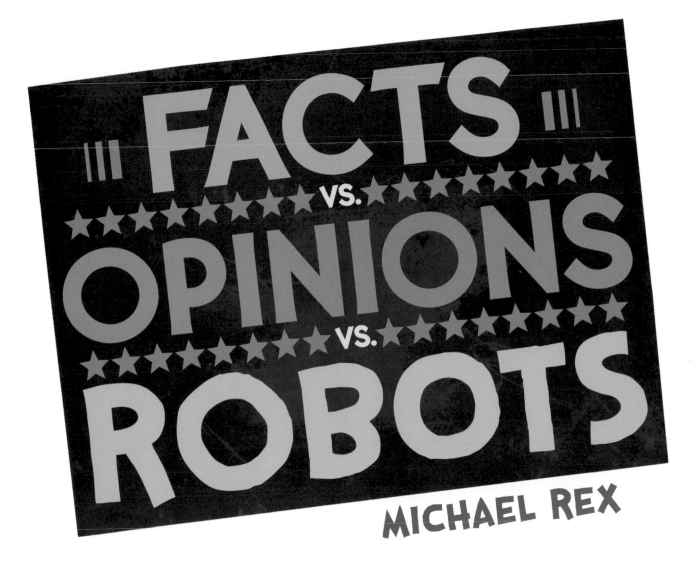

"FACTS" vs. OPINIONS vs. ROBOTS

MICHAEL REX

 Nancy Paulsen Books

To R2-D2, C-3PO,
Marvin, Bender, and RoboCop

NANCY PAULSEN BOOKS
An imprint of Penguin Random House LLC, New York

Nancy Paulsen Books is a registered trademark of Penguin Random House LLC.

Visit us online at penguinrandomhouse.com

Library of Congress Cataloging-in-Publication Data is available.

Manufactured in China by RR Donnelley Asia Printing Solutions Ltd.
ISBN 9781984816269
10 9 8 7 6 5 4 3 2 1

Design by Dave Kopka
Text set in Martin Gothic URW
The artwork was created 100% digitally using Photoshop.

Do you know the difference between a

FACT

AND AN

OPINION?

It can be a hard thing to understand.
Even these robots get confused.
But maybe if we work together,
we can figure it out.

Here are three robots.
Each robot has two eyes.
One robot is blue, one robot
is red, and one robot is yellow.

Are there three robots?
Do they each have two eyes?
Do any of them have three eyes?

Is one blue? Is one red? Is one yellow?
Is there a green robot?

Great! These are facts!
A fact is anything that can be proven

Now, let's try something different.

Which of these robots is the most fun?
The blue one, the red one, or the yellow one?

Good choice!
The choice you made was an

An opinion is something that you

FEEL AND YOU BELIEVE

but you cannot prove.

Opinions are wonderful and we all have them.
They are what make us

UNIQUE

But it is very important to know the difference
between a **FACT** and an **OPINION**.

There is only one robot here.
Is that a **FACT** or an **OPINION**?

The robot is green.
Is that a **FACT** or an **OPINION**?

Green is a good color for a robot.
Is that a **FACT** or an **OPINION**?

You're getting good at this!
Now, here's a hard one . . .
Is this a **BIG** robot?
Or a **MEDIUM** robot?
Or a **SMALL** robot?

Hmmmmmmmmm . . .
Without any other robots to compare,
we don't know if it's big, medium, or small.

So we must

WAIT

until we have
more information.

Now here come a few more robots, so we have more information. Is the green robot the biggest or the smallest?

No. It is a medium-sized robot. So that is a

Let's try some more...

Two of these robots have square heads,
and one has a round head.
Is that a **FACT** or an **OPINION**?

FACT!

Which robot would you like to be friends with?
Is that a **FACT** or an **OPINION**?

OPINION!

These robots like to dance.
Which of them has the coolest moves?
Is your choice a **FACT** or an **OPINION**?

OPINION!

One has two arms, and one has four arms.
Is that a **FACT** or an **OPINION**?

FACT!

Here is a new robot.
What is this robot's name?
Is it Bruno, Buddy, or Bubba?

Look closely at the picture.
Is there anything that proves his
name is Bruno, Buddy, or Bubba?
Nope. Not at all.

What do we do when we don't have enough
information to make a decision?

We **WAIT** until we have more information.

Now that we are all experts on **FACTS** and **OPINIONS**, let's see if the robots understand.

Is having a favorite flavor a **FACT** or an **OPINION**?

It's an **OPINION**, and these robots sure have strong opinions!

Are the robots fighting?
Is that a **FACT** or an **OPINION**?

FACT!

Let's repair the robots and
see if they can do better . . .

See how it helps to listen to each other's opinions?

Here are two more robots.
Let's see what happens with them . . .

Is the blue robot being a good friend?

By ignoring the opinions of others,
we can hurt their feelings.

Maybe the blue robot needs to be rebooted.

BEEP!

So you don't like
scary movies. I don't
like cute puppy movies.
Do you like space
movies?

Yes, I do!
I do like space
movies!

Yay, that reboot worked out well.

Now look who is back and wants to watch the movie.

Remember when we wanted to know
this robot's name? Is it Bruno, Buddy, or Bubba?

It's Bubba! That is now a

These robots have figured out a lot!
You see, when we respect the opinions
of others, we can all

GET ALONG

Now that we know the differences between **FACTS** and **OPINIONS**, it's important to remember that while we try not to argue about our opinions, we can't argue with

FACTS

Oh no! This is the last page of the book.
Is that a **FACT** or an **OPINION**?

Is this an awesome book?
Is that a **FACT** or an **OPINION**?

If you want, you can
read it again, and that's a

FACT!

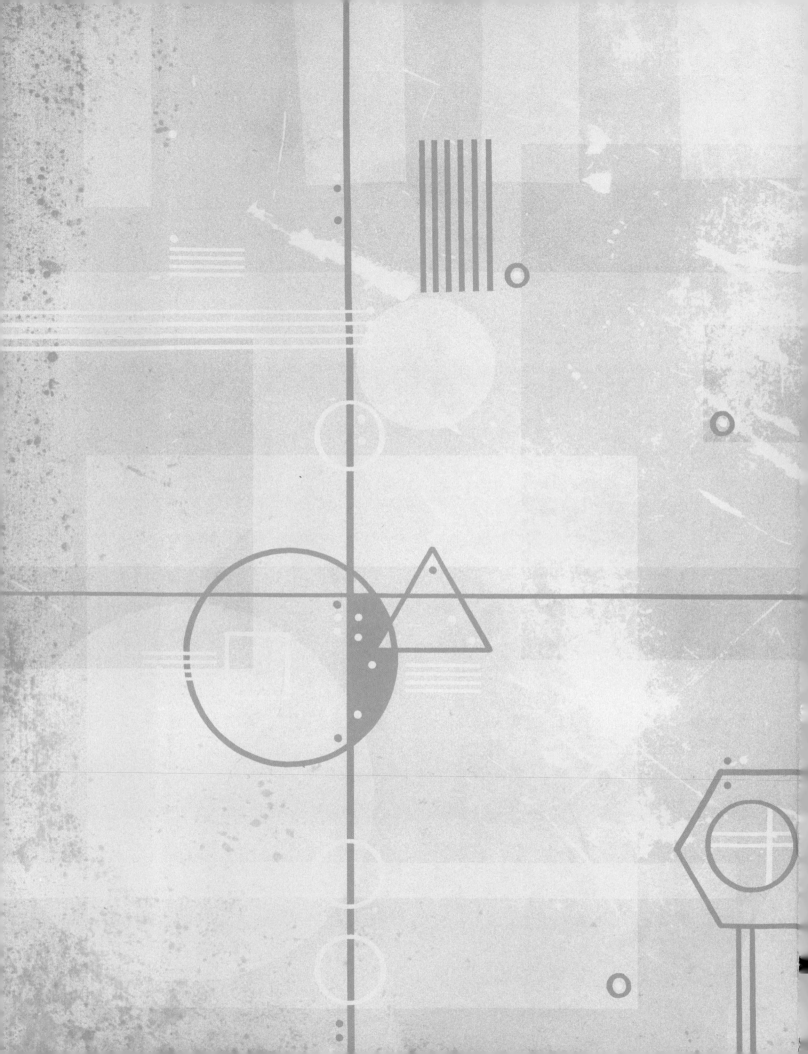